Original Korean text by Bo Rin

Illustrations by Yeong-jin Park

Korean edition © Dawoolim

This English edition published by big & SMALL in 2015
by arrangement with Dawoolim

English text edited by Joy Cowley

English edition © big & SMALL 2015

Distributed in the United States and Canada by
Lerner Publishing Group, Inc.
241 First Avenue North
Minneapolis, MN 55401 U.S.A.
www.lernerbooks.com

ISBN: 978-1-925233-69-8

Printed in Korea

What Lives in the Sea?

Written by Bo Rin
Illustrated by Yeong-jin Park
Edited by Joy Cowley

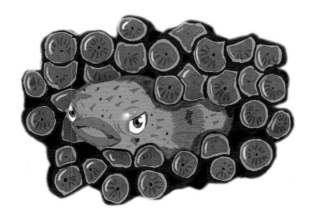

big & SMALL

The sea is full of remarkable creatures.
Each one is designed for the kind of life
it will live in the sea.

About 70 per cent of the Earth's surface is covered by sea.
It is the biggest habitat for life on Earth.

The **sea urchin** lives on the sea floor.

It has sharp spines and it feeds on seaweed.

If the **starfish** loses an arm, it can grow another.

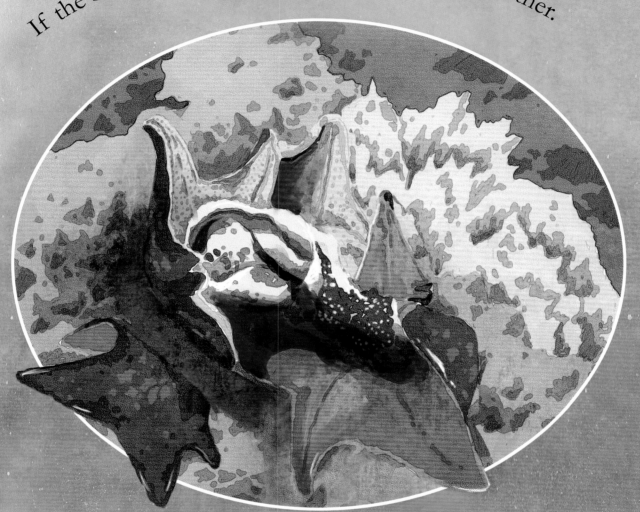

The starfish moves slowly, feeding on dead fish.

Each creature has its own way
of protecting itself.

The **octopus** has eight tentacles.

It squirts dark ink when it wants to get away.

This is a **butterfly fish** with an eye on its tail.

The fake eyes are to scare away big fish.

These creatures have other ways
of protecting themselves.
Some bite. Some sting.
Some have hard shells
and some swim very fast.

Can you work out
who does what?

15

A **crab** has claws that snip like scissors.

The shell is hard but the crab is soft inside.

Jellyfish float around looking like wobbly jelly.

But the long tentacles sting tiny fish.

Each creature has its own way
of finding and catching
the food that it needs.

The **stingray**'s mouth is underneath.

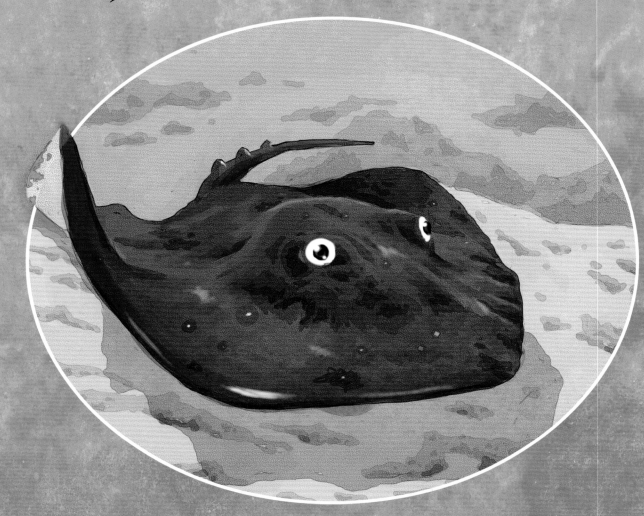

It eats small creatures hiding in the sand.

The **anglerfish** has a very big mouth.

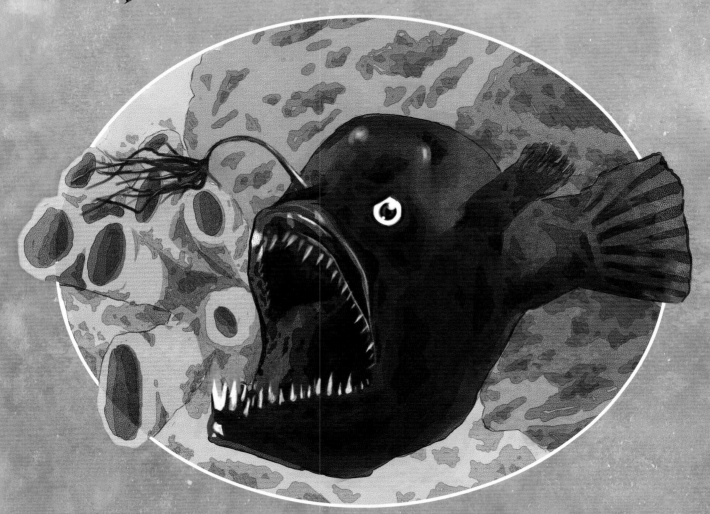

It scoops in little fish and eats them.

These creatures swim fast
to catch their prey.
Do you know what they are?

This is a big **blue whale.**

The **shark** does have teeth.

It does not have teeth.
It gulps down little shrimps.

It bites the prey it catches.

This little fish is hiding in the weed.

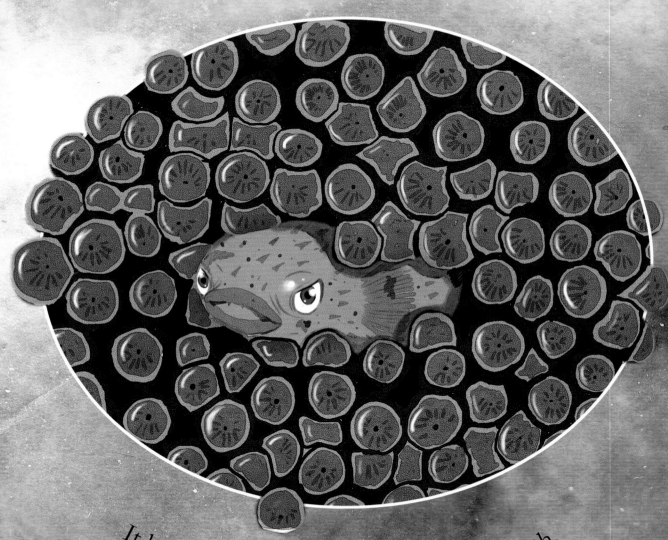

It has one upper tooth and one lower tooth.

Its mouth looks like the bill of a bird.

Why are the other fish afraid of it?

It can take in water and blow itself up.
Its spines are poisonous!

A porcupine fish!

Don't go near!

What Lives in the Sea?

The sea is the largest habitat on earth. Many different creatures live in the sea. Each has its own way of catching prey and protecting itself from enemies. All are perfectively adapted to their life in the sea.

Let's think

What are some of the creatures you can find in the sea? Make a list!

What are their characteristics?

How do they swim in the water?

How do they find and catch their food?

How do they protect themselves?

Let's Do!

Let's draw a picture showing some creatures living in the sea. Draw as many creatures as you can. Let's show the various characteristics of the creatures, the different depths at which they live, how they protect themselves and what they eat.